TIMMY
The West Coast Tug

by
Jeremy Moray

Illustrated by
Dee Gale

Harbour Publishing

AUTHOR'S NOTE

There are many individuals, companies and organizations to whom my thanks are due. But above all, to Gary Kleaman of Lionsgate Tug and Barge Ltd. Gary had to spend hours listening to my questions about "tugging," and then, with great patience, explain the answers in detail — though I believe he really enjoys recounting tug stories!

J.M.

Canadian Cataloguing in Publication Data

Moray, Jeremy, 1943–
　　Timmy the west coast tug

　　ISBN 1-55017-005-8
　　I. Gale, D.　II. Title
　　PS8576.　O73T5　jC813'.54　C80-091172-5
　　PZ7.M673Ti　1980

Published by
　Harbour Publishing Co. Ltd.
　P.O. Box 219
　Madeira Park, BC Canada V0N 2H0

Printed and bound in China through Colorcraft Ltd., HK

Tenth printing, 2004

for
Alexandra

ANOTHER AUTHOR'S NOTE

Don't forget to follow the story on the chart at the back of this book.

J.M.

It was a cold, clear morning in March. Timmy the Tug was snoozing quietly at his mooring in False Creek, right in the middle of Vancouver. Suddenly he was woken up by a loud squawk. It was his friend Simon the seagull, who lived under Granville bridge.

'Wake up, Timmy!' called Simon.

'Oh! Hey! What did you make that noise for?' Timmy jumped and sent little ripples scudding across the water.

'Just wanted to wake you up,' Simon laughed.

'Oh, well; I expect Captain Jones will be here soon to start work,' Timmy sighed.

Captain Jones was Timmy's owner. He looked after Timmy and drove him around. He was a kind, smiling man with a loud voice and lots of whiskers. He smoked a pipe and always wore an old peak-cap.

'Here he comes now,' called Simon, as he flew round in a circle above Timmy. 'And he's got Matilda with him. I think I'll go off and have some breakfast.' He flew away towards the big orange sun that was coming up over the mountains.

''Bye, 'bye, Simon,' Timmy called. 'See you out in the bay.'

Timmy smiled and bobbed up and down gently as Captain Jones and Matilda climbed onto his deck.

Matilda was a fat, grey cat with big green eyes. She went everywhere with Captain Jones. He and Timmy had rescued her when she had fallen off an Australian ship in English Bay two years ago. She was a very mischievous cat.

'Hello, Timmy,' boomed Captain Jones. 'It's time to get you warmed up.'

'Oh good!' said Timmy. 'I'm freezing.'

Captain Jones hummed to himself as he carried his kit bag into one of the cabins.

Behind his wheelhouse, Timmy had two cabins. One had two bunks in it where the crew could rest. The other cabin, called the galley, had a stove and a table with seats around it. Also there was a small storeroom which was next to the most important room of all, Timmy's engine room. It was so important that it had a special storm proof door. This was to make sure that no water would get near Timmy's engine, if he was sailing through rough seas.

Captain Jones came out of the cabin. He was wearing his sea boots, and bright yellow oilskins over his thick blue sweater. And of course, his old peak-cap.

'I hope you're ready for work, today, Timmy,' he called. He climbed up into the wheelhouse. 'We're going to haul a log-boom from Gambier Island all the way up to the mill at Powell River.'

'That's great,' thought Timmy. 'That means we'll be sailing at night.' 'I like sailing at night. When it's good weather, I can see all the stars, and sometimes the glowing moon.'

All this time, Matilda had been prowling around Timmy's decks. Before each journey, she liked to make sure everything was in order.

Soon Frank, Captain Jones' mate, arrived with the two deck hands John and Derek. Frank gave his kit bag to John to put in the cabin for him. Followed by Matilda, he climbed up into the wheelhouse where Mr. Jones was about to start Timmy's engine.

Timmy felt a lovely tingling feeling inside him as his electrics were turned on. Then his big, powerful engine roared into life.

'That's much better,' he thought. 'Now I can get warm, and then I'll be ready to go.'

He heard a crackling noise coming from the wheelhouse. Captain Jones was turning on the radio to get the weather report.

'Sounds like good weather all the way Captain,' Frank said. He laid out the charts on the chart table at the back of the wheelhouse.

'That's good. Let's get underway, then,' said Captain Jones as he went and stood behind the shiny wooden wheel.

John and Derek untied Timmy's ropes. Before long, he was chugging slowly under Burrard bridge and out into English Bay.

Once they had passed the Planetarium, Captain Jones put Timmy's engine at full speed ahead.

He set him on a course for Point Atkinson Light, which was flashing in the distance. Timmy loved going fast because he could make a big frothy bow wave in front of him.

'There's no better place in all the world to be a tug,' he shouted excitedly. He sped along between the huge ships anchored out in the bay.

But suddenly, he saw lots of big sailboats coming straight for him. They had huge coloured sails and were moving very fast. Closer and closer they came.

'Oh, no!' thought Timmy. 'We're in the middle of a sailing race. They might hit us!'

Matilda was crouching on the foredeck.

She let out a long, loud, meow, and put a paw over her head, as one of the boats sped past, very close to them.

Captain Jones saw what was happening. He steered Timmy carefully between two enormous ships, and out of the way of the racing sailboats.

'Jumping jellyfish!' exclaimed Timmy. 'That was scarey!'

Captain Jones laughed. 'Always try to keep out of their way whenever we can,' he said, and took a swig of tea from his big china mug.

Matilda looked up slowly, and whispered to Timmy, "I wasn't really frightened, you know.'

But Frank gave her a saucer of tea to calm her nerves, anyway.

'So there you are!' shouted Simon as he launched himself from the top of the Point Atkinson lighthouse. 'I thought you'd gone back to sleep.'

'Did you have a good breakfast?' Timmy asked, as Simon flew alongside him.

'Yes, thanks; I had a crab and six oysters — delicious! Good morning, Matilda,' Simon continued.

Matilda licked her lips hungrily when she heard Simon say this. But she didn't say hello to him. She just shut her eyes and flicked her tail. Matilda always pretended not to like Simon. But she was quite fond of him, really.

Captain Jones poked his head out of the window and called, 'Good morning, Simon. We're on our way to Centre Bay on Gambier Island to pick up a log boom. Coming with us?'

'That'd be great,' replied Simon. He flew down and settled on the top of Timmy's short mast.

They sped on into Queen Charlotte Channel. As they passed Whytecliff Point, Simon leapt into the air and shouted excitedly, 'Look, Timmy, there's the Nanaimo ferry, coming out of Horseshoe Bay.'

'Oh, yes,' replied Timmy. 'And look at all your friends following it.'

'I must go and see them,' said Simon as he flapped his big wings. 'My granny's going to Nanaimo today to see my aunt. Because she's getting old, she always follows the ferry. Then she can have a ride when she gets tired. I'll be back soon.'

Simon flew off and Timmy watched as he disappeared among the other seagulls.

'There he goes again,' Timmy thought to himself. 'He never sits still. Even when he isn't flying off somewhere, he's always hopping from one leg to the other and making funny gull noises. And he's always eating. Still, he is a good friend.' Timmy smiled to himself.

Matilda stretched, yawned and put her head between her paws.

They turned left round Hood Point and headed towards Gambier Island. It wasn't long before Simon was back.

'Granny's fine,' he said. 'As I got there, she was eating a hamburger bun that a child had given to her. Then she settled herself on one of the liferafts.' Simon chuckled as he landed on Timmy's bow.

'It's alright for some people,' muttered Matilda. 'If I went on a ferry, I'd have to stay on the car deck.'

'Cheer up, Matilda,' said Timmy. 'Not many cats get the chance to travel in luxury on a tug.'

John and Derek came out of the galley. They went back to the aft deck to get the towing line ready, and check the big green winch. Frank went into the storeroom. He brought out the lanterns, and the metal spikes that would hold them on the log boom.

And so, with Simon and Matilda standing proudly on the bow, Timmy entered Centre Bay. Captain Jones brought him slowly up to the log boom which was lying along the East shore. It was very long and made up of hundreds of logs. They were held together like a great big raft. Timmy was glad he had his big rubber tires all round his sides to protect him, as he nudged gently against it.

When they had stopped, Derek and John jumped onto the log boom. They hammered a metal lantern spike into the large log which lay across the front of the boom. As Frank handed them a lantern, Matilda jumped onto the logs. She wanted to chase some seagulls and crows that were sitting there. But Simon squawked loudly to warn the birds, and they all flew away. Matilda turned round and frowned at Simon.

'Spoil sport! Bird brain!' she growled, as she jumped back onto Timmy's deck. Flicking her tail crossly, she stalked off and sat on the cabin roof, and sulked.

Captain Jones took Timmy all the way down to the other end of the long boom. Frank fixed another lantern onto the last log.

'There you are, Timmy,' he said, as they steamed back to hitch the tow line to the front of the boom. 'Now the other boats can see where your tow is when it's dark.'

It wasn't long before everything was ready.

Simon flew up in the air and called: 'Clear the way! Here comes Timmy the tug with a log boom!'

Timmy heaved and strained. With his big propeller churning the water behind him, he moved very, very slowly out of Centre Bay.

'Well done, Timmy,' shouted Captain Jones, above the roar of the engine.

'He's a tough little tug,' said Frank.

'It's a bit difficult to get going,' panted Timmy. 'But once we're under way, it's much easier.'

As soon as they were out of the bay, Captain Jones told John to let out a long, long tow line. Now Timmy settled down to the journey ahead of him.

He liked pulling log booms. He could spend his time watching everything that was going on around him, as he chugged slowly along.

Timmy steamed down Barfleur Passage. As he passed the end of Keats Island, Simon flopped onto his deck.

'Where have you been?' asked Timmy.

'Sally the seal invited me to lunch at her home on Anvil Island.'

Sally was a very jolly, bouncy seal who loved parties. Almost every day she had friends over for lunch or dinner.

Simon straightened out his feathers as he settled down in a coil of rope on Timmy's foredeck.

'I think I've eaten too much,' he moaned. 'I'm going to have a sleep.'

Then he saw the cat lying nearby.

'Don't you pounce on me while I'm asleep, Matilda,' he said.

'Really, Simon, I couldn't be bothered,' said Matilda. She got up, stretched and padded off to see what else was going on. She found Frank polishing the brass rail that runs along the side of the cabins.

'You're always working,' she purred as she rubbed up against his legs.

'We have to keep Timmy looking smart,' replied Frank, bending down and stroking Matilda. 'In fact, he's known as the smartest tug on the West Coast.'

When he had finished his polishing, Frank said to Matilda: 'It's time for me to go and have a rest. I have to take over the helm from the Captain as soon as it gets dark.'

Matilda sneaked into the cabin behind him. She felt like having a nap, too.

With no one to talk to, Timmy sang to himself all afternoon as he chugged along. He passed several little boats fishing off Gower Point, and another tug came past him, pulling a barge full of wood chips.

Later, the sun sank towards the mountains on Vancouver Island. It was time for Captain Jones to turn on Timmy's navigation lights. Frank and Matilda got up after their rest. Frank went into the wheelhouse to talk to Captain Jones. Matilda thought she could hear supper being prepared. She went into the galley where John was busy making some soup. She jumped up onto his shoulder and sat there, staring hopefully into the pot, and purring loudly.

By now, Timmy was approaching White Islets.

Suddenly, they heard a lot of seagulls shouting and cheering.

'What's going on over there?' asked Captain Jones looking out of the wheelhouse window.

'I'll go and have a look,' called Simon, who had been woken up by the noise.

'All I can see is a lot of splashing in the water, and lots of Simon's friends jumping up and down on the big white rocks,' said Timmy looking over to his right.

Just then, Wally the Killer Whale surfaced beside Timmy. He squirted a big fountain of water high into the air. 'Hello, Timmy,' he said. 'Come to see my swimming team?'

So that was it. Wally was training his team of whales for a swimming match, and the seagulls were having great fun cheering them on. Round and round the island the whales swam, with Wally shouting advice and encouragement. Matilda joined Frank and Captain Jones in the wheelhouse. John and Derek came out on the deck. They all laughed and cheered as Timmy steamed slowly past.

Soon it was getting dark. As the light on the island began to flash, the whales and the seagulls set off for home. Simon flew back to join Timmy. When they had said goodnight to each other, Simon went to his favourite place to sleep. This was on the log boom beside one of the lanterns. There he could keep warm as Timmy pulled him along through the cold night.

As the stars twinkled above, Timmy could see the Merry Island lighthouse flashing in the distance ahead of him. He gave a big yawn, and went happily to sleep. And Frank took over the helm from Mr. Jones.

When Timmy woke up the next morning, he got a terrible fright. He thought someone had put up a wall of cotton wool in front of his eyes.

'Oh no!' he cried. 'It's a fog. A great thick fog! Now what are we going to do?'

Captain Jones came out of the cabin, and climbed up into the wheelhouse.

'This is no good, Frank,' he said. 'Here we are in the narrowest part of Malaspina Strait, and I can only just see Timmy's bows. You'd better keep sounding the horn, in case there are other boats around.'

'O.K., Captain,' said Frank, and he pulled a small lever and Timmy gave a loud 'toot'.

'We must keep going. We've got to get the boom to the mill this afternoon. The men are waiting for it.' Captain Jones opened the window and was about to peer out, when Simon stuck his head in.

'Good morning, Captain. It's a nasty fog, isn't it? But don't worry, I can help you through. The fog is thick down here, but it doesn't go up very high. I can fly above it and tell you where you are. I just had a look, and I can see the tall tank above Stillwater Bay. I'll go and get some of my friends to help.'

With that, Simon flew off to Hardy Island. He knew he would find lots of his friends having breakfast there.

In minutes, he was back. Seeing the tank on the shore, he led his friends down through the fog and they all settled round the edges of the log boom. Simon went and stood on Timmy's bows. He called to the gulls to take it in turns flying up to have a look around, and then to tell him which way to go.

Matilda didn't like all this excitement. She jumped up into the wheelhouse and sat next to Captain Jones. She tried to drink out of his mug of tea when he wasn't looking.

'Don't worry, Timmy; we'll get you through the fog safely,' Simon said as he patted Timmy with his wing.

'Thank you, Simon. I'm glad you can help. It's very frightening not being able to see where we're going.'

So with the seagulls popping up and down from the log boom and Simon calling directions to Captain Jones, Timmy was able to keep going as fast as he could through the fog.

They had just turned right round Grief Point, when the fog lifted, and the sun came out. Timmy was very happy to be able to see properly again. All the seagulls jumped up and down and cheered and clapped.

Simon thanked them all for their hard work and told them they could go home now. But they decided to stay for the rest of the journey. It was fun riding on a log boom.

Soon they were approaching the big pulp mill. Its tall chimneys were puffing out clouds of white smoke high above the town of Powell River.

'We're almost there,' said Captain Jones.

'Yes, thanks to Simon and his friends,' said Frank.

'And a very fine tug,' said Simon and he winked at Timmy.

'And what about me?' muttered Matilda, twitching her tail.

Derek laughed and said: 'Come on, you silly cat. Don't sulk. I'll get you a saucer of milk.'

Timmy watched the little tug coming out from the mill to help him put the log boom in the booming ground. Suddenly, he heard the radio crackle. A voice was telling Captain Jones that he and Timmy were needed, next, at Crofton Mill on Vancouver Island. They were to tow a barge full of machinery back to Vancouver.

But that's another story.